DISNEY · PIXAR

THE GOOD DINOSAUR

The Junior Novelization

randomhousekids.com

ISBN 978-0-7364-3140-8

Printed in the United States of America

10 9 8 7 6 5 4 3 2 1

DISNEY · PIXAR

THE GOOD DINOSAUR

The Junior Novelization

Adapted by Suzanne Francis

Illustrations by Sharon Calahan

Illustration Layouts by Erik Benson, Adam Campbell,
Valerie LaPointe, Austin Madison, Ricky Nierva,
Rosana Sullivan, J.P. Vine, and Alex Woo

Random House 🏠 New York

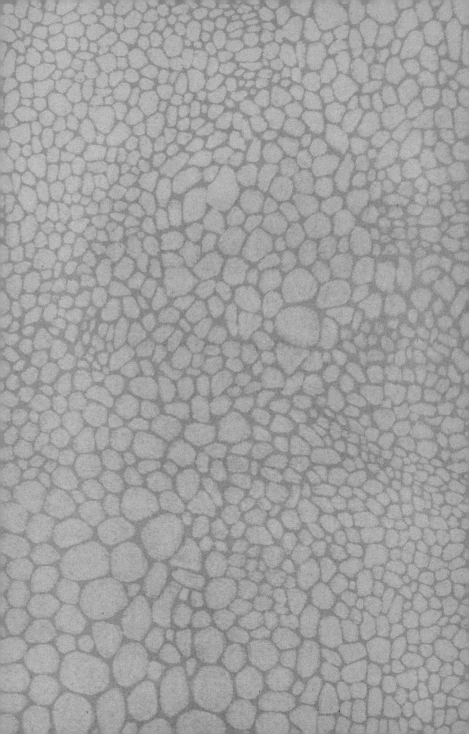

1

All was quiet on Earth 65 million years ago—on a day very much like many before it—as a group of dinosaurs peacefully ate in a lush green field. A big moon cast a gentle glow from above as they lazily chewed on fern fronds, twigs, and leaves.

But in the deepest, darkest depths of outer space— way beyond the dinosaurs—things were not so calm. A giant space rock was hovering millions of miles above Earth, moving more quickly than the others in the asteroid belt. It nudged a larger rock, sending an even bigger rock on its path. The asteroid began descending toward Earth. It burned as it entered the atmosphere, gaining momentum, on track to smack right into the blue planet. It raced faster and faster, getting closer and closer and closer, until . . .

Whooooosh!

The raging fireball darted right past Earth—just missing it.

Down below, the dinosaurs stopped chewing for a brief moment as they watched the bright silver streak of light shoot across the night sky.

Then they went back to chomping on their leafy greens.

Millions of years later, the world had changed. Earth and the dinosaurs that roamed it had become very different. Two Apatosauruses were busy cultivating a farm alongside a river at the base of a three-point mountain range called Clawtooth Mountain. Henry and Ida worked hard tending their fields and produced enough food to get themselves through every winter. Their farm was flourishing, and soon, they'd have a family.

Early one morning, Henry was outside doing his chores, using his mouth and long neck to spray streams of water across the cornfields, when he heard Ida's voice ring out: "Henry! It's time!"

Ida and Henry gazed at the eggs cozily sitting together in their large nest. All three were smooth and white, but one of them was quite a bit larger than the other two. Naturally, they assumed that would be their biggest and strongest. Ida and Henry had been dreaming about the little dinosaurs growing inside those beautiful eggs for so long. It was hard to believe the waiting was about to be over. They watched with hopeful eyes as one of the smaller ones wobbled just a bit. Then it wobbled a bit more. And finally . . . a tiny crooked opening formed.

Crackle. Crackle. Crack!

The shell split open and, like a little ray of sunshine, a female dinosaur poked her head out of the shell. The top of the egg fell to the ground, and with some effort, the baby dinosaur reached for it. Unfortunately, she was a bit off-balance and tipped right over. Momma and Poppa chuckled at their darling daughter.

Poppa reached down to lift the shell up, but the little dinosaur was nowhere to be found! He was worried at first, but then he heard the sweetest little laugh.

From out of nowhere, she appeared on Momma's back and let out a squeaky roar as she rode down her momma's long neck. Momma grabbed her baby by the tail before she hit the ground.

"You little sneak," Momma said lovingly.

The baby dinosaur laughed.

"Hello, Libby," Momma said.

Just then, the other small egg began to wobble. *Crack!*

A crack appeared at the top of its shell. It wobbled a bit more until . . . *Pop!* A foot pushed against the shell and came out!

Pop!

Pop!

Pop!

One by one, three more feet pierced through, sticking straight out. The egg rolled over and its four thick legs stomped around until it bashed into a log post. The shell crumbled away and a tough little male dinosaur—built like a tank—stood and looked at Momma and Poppa. His head was big for a baby Apatosaurus and looked as if it were balancing on top of his long neck.

"Hello, Buck," Poppa said proudly. The little dinosaur picked up a stick and started beating his father's leg with it. "He's got your eyes," he told Momma.

Momma and Poppa looked at the biggest of the eggs. They waited and waited, expecting their final child to emerge, but nothing happened.

All of a sudden, Buck appeared and started smacking the giant egg with a huge stick.

Poppa immediately intervened. "Get out of there, you little prickle bush," he said.

A crack slowly formed around the top of the egg.

Momma and Poppa leaned in. "All right, this is gonna be a big one!" Poppa said excitedly.

Crack!

The egg opened and the top popped off. Both parents gasped in anticipation, but nothing more happened. No little dinosaur emerged. They leaned forward, peering in, and curled up inside the bottom of the egg was the tiniest dinosaur either of them had ever seen!

Poppa pulled off the top half of the shell, and the tiny dinosaur timidly peeked out at them.

"Hello, Arlo," Poppa said, trying to coax the little Apatosaurus out of the egg. But Arlo didn't move. His arms and legs were splayed, gripping the inside of the shell tightly. He was not interested in leaving.

"Come on out," Poppa encouraged.

Arlo nervously inched forward, quivering with fear.

"Look at you," said Poppa, smiling adoringly.

Then Arlo tipped over and fell flat on his face with his backside sticking straight up in the air. Seeing a golden opportunity, Buck lumbered over and smacked Arlo on the butt with his stick.

"Buck!" scolded Poppa.

Buck scurried off, bouncing and romping about with Libby. Arlo watched them for a moment and then decided to join the fun. He was nervous at first, but as he picked up speed, he began to enjoy running around with his brother and sister.

Eventually, the three little dinosaurs ran all the way to the door, where the view stopped them in their tracks. Their eyes opened wide as they gazed out at the big, bright world outside. There was a large mountain range and fields that seemed to go on for miles.

"That's Clawtooth Mountain. And this is our farm," said Poppa contentedly. "We're all gonna take care of it together."

Libby and Buck already seemed excited by the farm and the possibilities that lay ahead of them. But Arlo was overwhelmed and unsettled by all of its newness and unfamiliarity. The tiny dinosaur trembled a little as he looked at the wide world that loomed in front of him.

By the time they were five years old, Buck, Libby, and Arlo were expected to help around the farm. Libby and Buck always did their chores—and they even knew how to have fun while doing them. Libby loved tricking Buck into doing her work for her.

One time, when she didn't particularly feel like watering the crops, she hid in the high stalks of corn with a mouthful of water. When Buck was within range, she aimed and took her shot . . . spraying him right in the face! Libby quickly retreated into the fields, laughing hysterically at her shocked brother.

Determined to get revenge, Buck ran to the trough

and filled his giant mouth with water. Libby peeked out from behind the corn and stuck her tongue out at him, then darted out of sight again.

In his attempt to hit her, Buck sprayed the entire field. Libby saw that each stalk had been watered, so she raced out. When Buck finally caught up to her, he hardly had any water left. He wound up only spraying her with a light drizzle.

With a big smile on her face, Libby called, "Momma! I finished my watering!" She turned to her brother. "Thanks, Buck," she teased.

Libby grinned as she watched Buck grudgingly begin his work.

But things were very different for Arlo. He struggled to find his place. Being smaller than his siblings didn't help matters, but Arlo's biggest problem was his fear. He was afraid almost all the time and of almost everything. And it held him back, making it difficult for him to accomplish even the simplest of chores.

One morning, Momma helped Arlo get ready to do

one of his dreaded daily chores: feeding the cluckers. He hated those birds. They made terrible noises, and he was sure they could pierce right through his foot with their sharp, hooked beaks. The way they looked at him with their cold, black eyes . . . it was like they were thinking up different ways to peck him to pieces. Just the thought of them sent a ripple of shivers down his spine.

"Can't I do somethin' else, Momma?" Arlo pleaded.

Momma smiled as she hung the basket of corn kernels around his neck and gently nudged him with her big tail.

"Get goin'," she chuckled. Reluctantly, Arlo headed off alone.

He slowed as he approached the fenced-in coop. As much as he hated all the noises those feathered fiends made, what was even eerier was the present silence. Carefully and quietly, he peeked inside, wondering where they were.

A sudden rustling in the grass startled him and he jumped, scattering some feed onto the ground.

"Who is that?" Arlo asked, looking toward the sound. He craned his neck through the grass and saw Eustice, a fuzzy little baby tangled up in some weeds. Relieved, Arlo bent down to help her. He peeled off the weeds, one by one.

As he freed Eustice, a pair of big, old, ugly clawed feet scratched into the ground beside him.

Squawk!

It was Henrietta, Eustice's scary momma!

Arlo screamed as Henrietta chased him away. She screeched and squawked, horrifying Arlo with each awful noise.

"Aaahhhhhhh!" Arlo screamed as he ran for cover.

In his panic, Arlo ran to the silo—where Poppa, Momma, Libby, and Buck were working. He curled himself up in Poppa's tail and closed his eyes. It was his favorite hiding spot.

Poppa unwound his tail and looked down at Arlo. "Is there a problem?" he asked calmly.

"Oh, that?" Arlo said, trying his best to hide his fear. "That was nothing—you know Henrietta."

Poppa chuckled. "You're okay."

Arlo watched as Poppa went back to work. He filled the silo with corn and closed up the opening with a boulder. Then he turned and faced the family.

"That should do it. This will keep them rotten critters from stealing our food," he said proudly.

Momma gazed lovingly at her husband. "Put your mark on there, Henry," she said. "You earned it."

The kids cheered. Then they waited eagerly to see what he would do next.

Poppa pushed his foot into a thick puddle of mud, making a footprint, and stamped his foot onto a rock. He lifted the printed rock and slid it into place—at the top of the silo. "There," he said, smiling. He turned to his wife and said, "You make your mark, Ida."

"What for?" she asked.

"Oh nothin', really," Henry said sarcastically. There was a smile on his face and in his voice as he continued: "You made the cabin, the fence, and three kids."

Momma smiled. "I am pretty impressive," she said

lightly. Then Momma made a mark, too, on the big boulder next to Poppa's.

All three kids excitedly charged toward the silo, shouting, "Me too! I'm doin' it! Mine's going to be the highest!"

Arlo moved toward the mud puddle first. He wanted to put his print up on the silo right away. Libby and Buck weren't far behind. All three of them wanted to participate in this special moment. But Poppa stopped them. "Now hold on. It's not that easy," Poppa explained. "You gotta earn your mark. By doin' something big, for something bigger than yourself."

All three kids gazed lovingly toward Poppa. It was clear they were really listening.

"Someday you'll all make your mark. And I can't wait to see it," Poppa concluded.

Arlo was inspired by Poppa's words. He looked up at Poppa's and Momma's footprints, imagining his up there, right next to theirs. He was determined to make his mark.

3

By the time they were ten years old, Libby and Buck both had their marks on the silo. Buck was super strong and was able to lift heavy things. He made his mark when he chopped down dozens of trees, making space for a new field of crops. Libby could plow nice, straight lines and made her mark when she plowed an entire field.

Arlo had yet to make his mark, and the gaping hole where his print was supposed to be was a constant reminder. As he grew, instead of having less fear, he seemed to be weighed down by it more and more.

Everyone expected him to make his mark by

successfully tackling his farm chore. But he always ended up running scared. It seemed that where Libby and Buck were able to succeed, Arlo was destined to fail. He felt terrible about it, and the knot in his stomach produced more anxiety and fear with each passing day.

Though hopeful and supportive, even Momma and Poppa started to grow a little concerned. "He'll get there," Poppa said.

One day, Arlo decided it was finally time for things to change. He was sick and tired of being the only family member without a mark. Arlo was determined to take on the cluckers and made a secret promise to himself that he would finish the job—by any means necessary.

I'm bigger than them, I'm bigger than them, he thought over and over, trying to fight off his fears with positive thinking. He took a deep breath and went into the coop, armed with corn kernels and ready to do something big!

Once inside, Arlo tried to intimidate the cluckers.

"I hope you have strong stomachs, 'cause you're about to get fed!"

But just as Arlo started to scatter the feed, he heard a voice in the distance.

"Arlo?" it whispered.

He followed the sound of his name and found Buck outside and in bad shape. He was lying down in the grass and looked like he'd been beaten up.

"Buck! What happened?" Arlo exclaimed.

"There were too many. Then they attacked," Buck said. He coughed, and Arlo could feel the panic begin to flood through his veins.

"You're gonna be okay," Arlo said.

"Sweet brother, tell the world how amazing I was," he whispered. With that, Buck closed his eyes and his head rolled to the side. Arlo was convinced his brother had just died—right in front of him.

"I'll go get help!" Arlo screamed.

Then a shadow began to slowly rise behind Arlo. He turned around and saw his worst nightmare: a giant clucker! Arlo tried to run away but tripped and fell hard to the rough ground.

Then he heard something even more unsettling. Someone was laughing at him. It was Buck! He'd put a clucker costume on his tail and used it to frighten the life out of Arlo.

"Oh, you should see your face," he howled.

Once he could breathe again, Arlo's whole body burned with an intense anger. He furiously launched himself at Buck, attacking him. "I should've known! You always gotta mess me up!" Arlo screamed.

"Me?" Buck asked. Then he effortlessly threw Arlo to the ground. "You mess up your chores and everyone else's!"

As they wrestled, Libby, Momma, and Poppa ran outside.

Arlo tried to get up again, and Buck moved as if to smack him. Arlo flinched, anticipating the hit, but Buck only chuckled. "You're such a coward," he said.

Momma and Poppa followed the sounds of the scuffle. They made their way toward the sound of the fighting brothers. "Buck!" Poppa yelled, causing

Buck to back off.

Arlo sat up. "I ain't a coward!" he yelled, holding back tears. "And I'm gonna make my mark, just like him and you and everybody!"

"You will, darlin'. You just need a little more time," Momma said gently.

Arlo stared at the ground, feeling low. "Forget it," he said, walking off. "I didn't even want that dumb mark anyway."

Momma and Poppa shared a concerned look.

"We gotta do somethin', Henry," Momma said quietly.

"I got an idea," Poppa said.

That night, while everyone was sleeping, Poppa gently woke Arlo. "Come with me," he whispered.

Arlo rubbed his eyes and groggily followed Poppa outside, where they stood in a field surrounded by darkness.

Even though he was with Poppa, Arlo didn't like being out there at night. He heard wild animals in the distance. And the dark, jagged edges of Clawtooth Mountain looked like they could chomp down on the whole farm at any moment. Arlo wanted to go back inside, but Poppa insisted he stay. "Okay, now take a walk out there," he said, nodding toward the field with his long neck.

"By myself?" Arlo asked nervously.

"Go on," Poppa encouraged.

Arlo went and stood in the middle of the big, open field. An ugly bug landed on his nose and he whimpered with fear. "Poppa!" he whispered urgently. Arlo's stomach lurched. He was paralyzed.

Suddenly, Poppa was at Arlo's side. He calmly and gently blew on the bug. It pulsed with light—it was a firefly! Relieved, Arlo smiled and stared at the glowing bug on his nose with wonder. Then it spread its wings and took flight, flashing into the night.

Poppa faced Arlo. "Sometimes you gotta get through your fear to see the beauty on the other side," he said earnestly.

Then Poppa slowly brushed his tail across the grass, sweeping it this way and that. Like magic, hundreds of fireflies slowly rose up out of the grass, flickering their beautiful yellow lights. It was incredible!

Arlo repeated Poppa's words to himself, trying to set Poppa's advice permanently into his mind. He wanted to remember them, but more than that, he wanted to be able to do it. He wished that he could be less fearful; he wished he could be more like Poppa.

Then, wanting to try Poppa's trick, Arlo ran through the field, forcing more fireflies to float up, flickering and flashing.

Arlo and Poppa continued and the two painted beautiful arcs and spirals of light against the dark sky. Arlo looked up at big, strong Poppa and smiled.

In the stillness, Poppa turned to his son. "Arlo, I've got a new job for you tomorrow. That is, if you still wanna make your mark."

Arlo smiled with anticipation. He wanted that mark, all right. He wanted it more than anything in the whole world. And he couldn't wait to see what Poppa had in store.

4

The next day, when Poppa and Arlo went out to the silo, they found corn scattered all over the ground.

"A dang wilderness critter's coming over the fence, getting into our silo, and eating our food. And I've had it up to my snout," Poppa said angrily. He knew that if the family didn't have enough corn for the winter, they would struggle to survive. Poppa turned to Arlo. "That's why *you're* gonna catch that critter."

Arlo smiled as he imagined his print up on top of the silo. He was ready!

Poppa collected some supplies and showed Arlo how to build a trap. He tied a rock to one end of a long rope, set up a net, and had Arlo place a pile of corn on the ground for bait.

When they were finished, he rolled a pumpkin onto the pile to show Arlo how the trap worked. The pumpkin snapped up the rope, and the net fell to the ground as a jingling sound rang out. Then Poppa picked up a huge mallet. "This is how you're gonna finish the job." He brought the mallet down fast, smashing the pumpkin to a pulp. "When that critter's taken care of, you'll put your mark on the silo, right next to mine."

Arlo's eyes lit up. "I'll take care of that critter, Poppa. It won't stand a chance."

Arlo then stood guard, pacing back and forth in front of the silo, waiting for the critter to fall into the trap. He tried to mentally prepare for his big moment, taking lots of deep breaths and telling himself over and over that he could catch the critter . . . and finish it off.

A bug flew by his face and he scowled at it. "What are you doing, you *bug*?" Arlo said, practicing his tough voice and his ninja moves. "Get out of here!"

He continued pacing, preparing, and trying not to let fear into his thoughts. When a rogue leaf crossed his path, he made sure it knew its place. "Move along, leaf!" he shouted. "Move along!"

Just then, Arlo heard the jingling sound of the trap. His heart leaped. He felt a rush of anxiety and a fluttering of fear. He had caught something! He had caught the critter!

Holding the mallet high above his head, Arlo approached, preparing to whack the trapped pest. "Y-y-you're dead, critter," he stuttered.

Arlo couldn't help but pause at the sight. What looked like a critter to Arlo was actually a human boy. The critter was choking from the net around his neck and struggling to breathe. And even though Arlo knew it was his job to catch the critter, he felt sorry for it. It was a living thing, and it just wasn't in Arlo's heart to bring the mallet down. Arlo sighed and opened the trap, releasing his caught critter.

"Okay . . . you're free," said Arlo, hoping it would

just run off. But the boy stared at him and then started walking toward him!

"Wh-wh-what are you doing?" Arlo asked, trying to back away. "Just—just leave! Flee!"

But the boy continued to investigate, sniffing and sniffing. Arlo was afraid. He felt like he was about to be attacked! Finally, he tripped over a rock and screamed. This startled the critter, and he took off into the high grass.

Hearing Arlo's cries, Poppa rushed over—just in time to see the wild pest escaping into the wilderness. "ARLO!" Poppa scolded. "Why'd you let it go?"

"It was bitin', comin' at me, and screechin' . . . and I—" Arlo stammered.

"You had a job to do!" Poppa yelled. He looked around and saw the critter's tracks leading into the wilderness. "You gotta get over your fear, Arlo, or you won't survive out here," he said firmly. "Come on. We're gonna finish your job right now."

Poppa pushed Arlo along, and they walked up to the fence. Then Poppa climbed over. To Arlo, it was as if Poppa were climbing right into the mouth of that terrible beast. The towering trees, the darkness, the rushing river, the wild animals . . . all just waiting to swallow them up. Plus, it had started to rain.

"Out there?" Arlo asked nervously, his mouth going dry.

Poppa turned to Arlo. "Let's go. Get over," he said.

Poppa was tired of Arlo's excuses. Poppa pushed Arlo over the fence with his tail, and the two went in search of the critter.

5

As they started toward the mountain pass, Arlo felt a giant lump growing in his throat. Fear seemed to take over his entire body. Even though he was with Poppa, he had never been so scared.

The wind moved noisily through the trees and caused branches to bend and sway. The rain was heavy now. Arlo looked at the sky. Dark storm clouds seemed to be swirling in, and he started to feel even worse. "Poppa, what if we get lost?" he asked, glancing around at the strange surroundings.

But Poppa wasn't stopping for anything. "As long as you can find the river, you can find your way home," he said plainly. Arlo nodded.

BOOM!

Thunder rumbled and popped in the distance as Poppa continued to push Arlo along. "What do you see?" he asked.

Arlo was confused and afraid. At first he didn't see anything. Then he looked down and tried to concentrate. "Uh, uh, t-t-tracks?" Arlo said.

"And they're washing out," Poppa said. "We gotta move." As the rain fell, water began to fill the critter's tracks in the mud—making them disappear.

"We're losing that critter!" cried Poppa, picking up speed.

Arlo tried to keep up with him.

CRACK!

Lightning flashed, causing Arlo to whimper. The thunder was louder now, and the storm was absolutely terrifying!

Trying to keep up, Arlo slipped in the mud and tumbled to the ground. "Poppa!" Arlo called. "Wait!"

At first, Poppa didn't turn around. "Arlo, what did

I say about—" But when he saw his son struggling and limping, he softened. "It's okay, Arlo. It's okay," he said kindly. "I just wanted you to get through your fear. To know that you can."

"But I'm not like you—" Arlo cried in frustration.

"You're me," Poppa said, smiling. "And more."

Crack!

BOOM!

Lightning flashed again, and the thunder grew even louder. The storm seemed to be right on top of them. Arlo leaned against Poppa, desperate for comfort. Poppa helped Arlo up and out of the mud. "I think we went far enough for today. Whaddya say we head home?" he asked.

As they started back, the ground trembled and the river swelled. Arlo could hear the ripping, crunching sound of roots coming out of the ground, and the loud thumping of trees falling against the wilderness floor in the distance.

Suddenly, Poppa's face showed alarm and he yelled, "Arlo, move!" He pushed Arlo up the hill with all his might, trying to get him away from the river. But Arlo's feet sank into the wet, thick mud as Poppa yelled, "Run!"

Horrified, Arlo looked upriver and saw something huge and black coming toward them. The wind whipped faster, stinging Arlo's eyes and knocking down trees so close that the sound of them hitting the ground was deafening. The thunder and lightning intensified. Arlo froze. He was unable to move.

All at once, the river water seemed to rise to the sky and roared toward them like a monster. Using all his might, Poppa pushed Arlo up to safety. Arlo watched helplessly as Poppa tried to get up the hill and slipped—just as the giant wall of water hit. Arlo cried out. The water swallowed Poppa and swept him away.

Arlo stared at the raging river as it became a colorless blur. The trees, the sky, and the earth beneath his feet seemed to melt away. He felt an indescribable hollowness.

Poppa was gone.

6

After that day, everything changed. The family worked hard, trying to keep up with the endless tasks that were necessary to maintain the farm. But as winter approached, they were falling behind. Momma was exhausted, and many of the fields were left fallow. The family worried they wouldn't have enough food to make it through the winter.

Arlo couldn't help but feel that it was entirely his fault. He had been the one to set the critter free. He had been the reason Poppa went into the wilderness that night. If he had just taken care of that critter, Poppa would still be alive and everything would be okay.

Momma carried a huge load of corn to the silo, but she was struggling. Arlo ran up to help her.

"You need to rest, Momma," he said.

"If we don't get this harvest in before the first snow, we won't have enough food for winter," Momma said desperately. "I know it's hard without Poppa. But I need you to do more, Arlo."

He picked up the load of corn and put it on his back. He smiled at her. "Don't worry, Momma. I won't let us starve."

"You're a good son," Momma said.

Arlo wavered, carrying the weight of the corn on his back. He could feel his legs wobble, but he was determined to make it.

When the silo finally came into view, he gazed at Poppa's mark and felt a familiar sadness wash over him. But he knew he couldn't stop to feel sad. He had to keep working.

Arlo walked carefully to the silo and slowly removed a rock to place the corn inside. He set the corn down and began to husk it, peeling each ear and tossing it into the silo. Then he heard something rustling inside and went to investigate. He saw a figure chomping the corn and spitting out the empty cobs.

When Arlo peeked inside, he couldn't believe his eyes: it was that pest from the trap! Arlo caught him red-handed.

"You!" With fire and rage in his heart, Arlo shouted, "My Poppa would still be alive if it weren't for you! It's all your fault." He lunged toward the critter and tried to bite him.

But the boy was too fast. He jumped on Arlo's neck and slid down toward his back—where the boy grabbed a stalk of corn and took off. Arlo chased him as he ran toward the river.

When Arlo caught up, he chomped down hard on the other end of the stalk, lifting the boy high in the air. The boy jumped down and scurried out of sight. But Arlo wasn't giving up. He continued in pursuit of the thief, with the stalk of corn remaining in his mouth.

Out of nowhere, the boy jumped from a tree,

growling, "Grrrrrrrrrrr!" He lurched toward the corn, bit down, and began to gnaw on the cob. He growled again—ferociously with a wild, hungry look in his eyes. Arlo swatted and spun around, trying to get the boy off, but he wouldn't let go. As Arlo twisted and twirled, he became dizzy and fell backward, plunging into the river!

The critter went flying, and Arlo lost track of him when he went under. Arlo gasped for air as the raging water overtook him. "Help!" Arlo screamed. He called for Momma, but the sound was muffled as his mouth filled with water.

The strength of the current carried him away so quickly that no one could hear his cries. In an instant, he was farther from home than he had ever been.

Arlo struggled to stay afloat, gasping for air as the rapids pulled him under. His body bashed against sharp rocks at the bottom of the river, scraping into his skin. Suddenly, a giant boulder came into view and Arlo whimpered, struggling to avoid it. But the river was much stronger than he was.

BAM.

His head slammed right into the massive rock. His vision became blurry, and he could barely make out Clawtooth Mountain as it disappeared into the distance.

Then everything went black.

7

Eventually, dazed and achy, Arlo opened his eyes and looked around. His legs were still in the water, and his body was beached on a small sandbar. He was miles down the river and very far from home.

Some big logs were jammed together next to him, making sharp peaks that looked like angry teeth. His body throbbed with pain, each scrape and scratch burning as he breathed. He felt the bump on his head and shuddered.

As Arlo took in his surroundings, fear began to ripple through his body. "Momma!" Arlo cried. "Momma!" His voice echoed, ringing against the towering cliff walls that rose all around him. When he quieted, the only other sound he could hear was the wind moving through the pine trees and the gurgles of the river washing over the rocks. He was completely alone.

Arlo gathered the strength to climb out and slowly rose to his feet. But the ground crumbled beneath him. He slipped and his jaw smacked against a boulder. Arlo lay still, trying to catch his breath. He needed to figure out what to do next.

Arooowwwwh. A loud howl sounded down in the canyon. He looked up toward the top of the cliff wall and saw . . . the boy from the trap! A burning anger boiled up inside of him. "You!" he yelled. "I should have killed you the first time!"

Furious, and fueled by his anger, Arlo propelled his body up the cliff to try to get to the boy.

The boy just sat on the edge of the cliff. Cocking his head this way and that, he watched curiously as Arlo clumsily made his way up the cliff wall. Arlo was working hard and struggling for breath, but he still managed a few choice words: "This is all your fault!"

The boy remained calm, sitting and watching. This made Arlo even angrier. He snapped. "Get over here!"

Then the boy did something entirely unpredictable: he tried to climb on Arlo's face!

"Get away!" Arlo screamed. He repeated it over and over, harshly jerking his neck and tossing the boy off. The boy turned and used his hind legs to kick dirt at Arlo's face. The dinosaur spit and coughed, trying to get the dust and dirt out of his mouth.

When Arlo finally managed to hoist himself up onto the cliff's edge, the boy had disappeared. "That's right! You better run!" Arlo called after him threateningly.

Arlo took a deep breath and slumped. He looked around at his surroundings again. The wilderness seemed to be the whole world. He couldn't see an end to it. He spotted a high ridge off in the distance. If he could get up to the ridge, maybe he could see where home was. With no choice, no one to ask, and no other ideas, he started off toward it.

8

Arlo climbed up to the top of the ridge and looked out. "Where am I?" he asked himself, looking in every direction. The lump in his throat returned. "Where's home?" he whispered, breathing heavily. He was trying not to panic. But he couldn't see Clawtooth Mountain anywhere. Stretched before him were miles and miles of trees, shrubs, boulders, and hills. The vastness of it all made him feel like a tiny speck. Nothing looked familiar. Even the river looked different. And it appeared to go on forever.

The river!

"As long as you can find the river, you can find

your way home," Arlo said to himself, remembering Poppa's words. He slowly trekked down toward the river.

There was no simple, clear path to walk. Arlo had to traipse around fallen trees with sharp, jagged branches. He walked cautiously, listening to the strange sounds of the wilderness. It took all his courage to focus on slowly putting one foot in front of the other.

After walking for a bit, Arlo noticed smashed berries scattered around and gasped in excitement. He looked up, and there, on a nearby hillside, he noticed a tree covered with berries.

Arlo was starving. He'd never been so hungry, or so happy to see a berry tree. He saw an angled boulder and balanced himself on top, leaning out to try and get one of the juicy berries. The boulder tilted, but he managed to catch himself, straddling the tree. Craning his neck out as far as he could, he reached, leaned, and stretched every part of his body. He even stuck his tongue out toward the branch, but he was unable to get to it. He took a deep breath and blew, causing the branch to swing toward him and . . . Sweet joy! He managed to bite a juicy berry right before . . . *BAM.* He lost his balance and fell, landing on his leg!

Frustrated, he tried to pick himself up but couldn't. His foot was buried under a pile of rocks wedged up against the boulder! He tried and tried, but he just couldn't break free. He was completely stuck.

Eventually, darkness fell over the wilderness. And like most things, it became even scarier without the light of day. Arlo didn't want to give up. He'd worked hard to pull himself free, leaving tracks in the ground as proof. But he was starting to lose hope. The nighttime sounded much louder than the daytime, with many different animals and insects screeching and chirping. Frightened, tired, hungry, and unable to move, Arlo had no choice but to cover his head and try to block it all out. He curled up and closed his eyes.

9

PSHHHHHH! The sound of shooting geysers woke Arlo. Groggy, he looked around, trying to remember where he was and what had happened.

When he finally did remember, he looked down at his foot. All of the rocks had been cleared away. He was no longer stuck! Arlo looked around and was stunned when he saw human tracks in the mud. He wondered if the boy had pushed the rocks away while he was asleep. Could that critter have done something to actually help Arlo? Even if he had, it wouldn't matter. Arlo was still angry; he forced the thought out of his mind and pressed on, walking along the river.

Drip.

Drop.

Drip.

Drop.

Cold raindrops began to fall from the sky. At first, Arlo felt as if he could hear each drop falling against the leaves, with their soft pitter-patter. But the rain quickly picked up, and in no time the pitter-patter turned into a constant stream, soaking everything and softening the ground. Thunder rumbled in the distance, and little creatures scurried about as they ran for shelter. The rain came down even harder and Arlo shivered, cold and wet.

BOOM!

A loud clap of thunder startled him. The storm was getting worse. Arlo collected some sticks and tried to build a shelter.

He leaned the bundle of thick sticks against each other, and they instantly collapsed to the ground.

"Arghhh," Alro grumbled.

He tried again.

Nearby, creatures were nestled in their cozy dwellings, safe and dry. A twitching nose with little whiskers peeked out from inside a hollow log. A small brown animal snored from his hole beneath a boulder. A bird sat comfortably inside her sheltered nest. It seemed all the little creatures fit neatly and comfortably into their tiny dry homes. One of them watched as Arlo struggled, trying to get his stick-shelter to work. Once Arlo managed to get the sticks balanced, he sat inside and stuck his tongue out at the creature. He was proud of himself.

Drip.

Drip.

Seconds later, raindrops dripped through the shelter and right onto Arlo's face. The creature squeaked, almost like it was laughing. Then it disappeared. When the creature returned, it had brought friends, and they all watched. They squeaked, staring at Arlo as if he were their evening entertainment.

Too tired, wet, and hungry to care, Arlo groaned. He decided to try and rest while the rain poured

down, soaking him and everything around him.

Then some shrubs nearby rustled. Arlo sat up, anxiously looking around for the source of the noise. He began to breathe rapidly as he became more and more nervous. The noise was coming closer and closer. The bushes stopped moving for a moment and suddenly, the boy from the trap came prancing out from behind them.

"You again!" Arlo said, infuriated.

The boy held a lizard in his mouth. He dropped it on the ground in front of Arlo, offering it to him. But Arlo wasn't interested. "Get outta here!" Arlo yelled. The boy backed up and carefully watched Arlo, as if waiting for something to happen. Arlo wondered what the boy expected him to do. Still alive, the lizard hopped up and quickly scurried away. The boy scampered off again, leaving Arlo in his shelter. As the setting sun turned the sky a dusty shade of pink, Arlo fell asleep.

The sound of the boy growling woke Arlo from his slumber. The boy appeared again, only this time he was dragging a huge, ugly bug toward Arlo. The boy flipped the bug on its back and signaled to Arlo. But Arlo was confused. What did the boy want him to do? Eat the bug? Arlo was disgusted. The boy sat still and stared—as if he were trying to read Arlo's expression.

Then the boy ripped the bug's head off with his teeth! He spit it out and tossed it aside, then dropped the bug's lifeless body in front of Arlo. He stepped back, waiting and watching him again.

Arlo was horrified. Repulsed by what he'd just seen, Arlo grabbed a branch and swept the bug away; he didn't want any part of the boy's headless bug.

The boy barked and ran off.

Moments later, berries dropped to the ground in front of Arlo. The dinosaur was skeptical, but he was also starving. He quickly ate a few berries but said, "I told you to . . . STAY—AWAY—FROM—ME!"

The boy climbed up on top of a boulder and watched dutifully as Arlo devoured every last berry.

"I'm still going to squeeze the life out of you . . ." He paused to reconsider his position for a moment. Arlo was still hungry, and he'd already eaten all the berries the boy brought. "But before I do, could you find me some more?" The boy didn't seem to understand. "You know . . . um . . . nom nom nom," Arlo said, and then he pretended to chew on a branch.

The boy grabbed the other end of the stick with his mouth and started pulling, playing tug of war. "No . . . no . . . Stop!" Arlo scolded, letting go of the stick. The boy gnawed on the stick and then took off with it!

"Hey, wait!" yelled Arlo. Curious, he followed the boy as he rushed off with the stick. Arlo watched from a distance as the boy dug a hole and placed the stick inside, burying it. The boy spit and kicked dirt over it to fill it back up. Then the boy ran off again.

Arlo wondered what the boy was thinking. He was starting to get frustrated. "You don't even know what you're doing," he said angrily. But he continued to follow the boy.

The boy jumped onto a nearby tree and nimbly ran across a branch like a squirrel. Arlo followed as the ground beneath him got narrower and narrower. Soon Arlo found himself on a cliff ledge! He started to panic, looking at the deep drop below, rocks crumbling beneath him. The boy stood for a moment, trying to figure something out.

"I knew it!" Arlo yelled, breaking the silence. "I'm gonna die out here because of you!"

The boy turned to Arlo and started to push his feet out. Arlo tried to keep his balance, but he was very wobbly. The boy scampered to the other side of Arlo and shoved him toward the cliff edge!

"No, no, no. Stop! Stop! STOP!" Arlo screamed as he lost his balance and fell forward. His feet stayed on the ledge, but his body fell over the ravine. He crashed onto the ledge on the other side, landing on his teeth! Arlo was now stretched out, connecting the two cliff edges over the ravine, like a giant dinosaur bridge!

Excitedly, the boy rambled across Arlo's body to get to the other side. "Why, you little . . . come back here!" Arlo growled through clenched teeth.

But the boy kept going, sniffing the ground and searching. Finally, the boy's body quivered and his foot tapped repeatedly against the ground, beating it like a drum.

"Heh-heh-heh-heh," he panted excitedly, and looked back at Arlo. He seemed to be gesturing toward a bush.

Arlo followed the boy's gaze and instantly understood. "Berries!" Arlo joyfully exclaimed, seeing thousands of juicy berries covering the bush. The glorious sight of food gave Arlo a sudden burst of energy, and he was able to propel his body up to the ledge. He ran toward the bush, chuckling with delight.

The boy pounced in front of Arlo and started to growl and bark. "What's with you?" Arlo asked. "We found them. They're right here." He continued toward the berries, and the boy growled and barked louder and louder. "Crazy critter," Arlo muttered, breaking off a branch of the berry bush.

Hisssss!

All of a sudden, a venomous snake fell out of the bush and landed right in Arlo's face! Arlo screamed. Then the ground beneath him crumbled, and he plunged down off the cliff, crashing into trees and cracking branches along the way.

As he hit the ground, Arlo groaned in pain. He tried to get his bearings, but the snake rose right up in front of him, hissing and ready to attack! Arlo gasped.

"Ahhhhh!" he screamed. He was terrified!

In a flash, the boy appeared in front of Arlo, growling at the snake! The snake lunged at the boy, but he instinctively jumped out of the way and managed to get behind it. Then the boy grabbed the snake and started gnawing on its scaly skin! With one last strike, the boy bashed his head into the snake, causing it to fearfully slither away. Arlo quickly got up and ran to the boy, who panted excitedly. Arlo couldn't quite believe it, but the little critter seemed happy to have protected him.

Arlo and the boy were walking along the river when they heard a strange voice call to them from behind the trees.

"Hello."

Arlo looked around, timidly. "Hello?"

"We've been watching you," the voice said.

Arlo walked toward the voice and saw a collection of creatures perched on the branches of a tree. They were all staring directly at him.

"We thought you were going to die," the voice said.

Arlo still couldn't tell where the voice was coming from. He searched the animals in the branches, trying to figure it out. He kept looking.

"But then you didn't," the voice said.

Finally, two eyes appeared, revealing a Styracosaurus with big branchlike horns. Small creatures of all sorts perched on the outstretched horns. The dinosaur took a step forward, abandoning the camouflage created by the woods.

His name was Forrest Woodbush, and he was a collector of pets. The animals sitting in his horns were his friends, and they protected him from the wild.

"That creature protected you," Forrest said. "Why?"

"I—I don't know. I'm going home," Arlo said. "Do you know how far Clawtooth Mountain is?"

The red bird sitting in Forrest's horn chirped, and he responded, "Good idea . . ." Forrest turned back to Arlo. "We want him."

"Wh-why?" Arlo asked.

"WHY? 'Cause it's terrifying out here. He can protect me, like my friends." Forrest introduced all the creatures to Arlo, explaining how each one helped to keep him safe in the wilderness. He pointed to a slothlike creature first. "This is Fury. He protects me from the creatures that crawl in the night."

Then he pointed to a furry critter. "This is Destructor. She protects me from mosquitoes."

Next, he pointed to the cutest, big-eyed creature of the bunch. "This is Dreamcrusher. He protects me from having unrealistic goals," he explained.

Finally, he pointed to the red bird. "And this is Debbie." She chirped again, and Forrest nodded. He said firmly to Arlo, "We need him."

"W-wait," Arlo said. "He—he's with me."

"If he's with you, what is his name?"

"His name? I—I don't know," Arlo answered.

"Hmmm . . . then I will meditate on this." Forrest calmly closed his eyes for a moment. He opened one and quickly blurted, "I name him. I keep him."

Forrest continued to hum, closing his eyes and shouting out names as they came to him. "Mmm . . . Killer!"

All eyes darted toward the boy. He gave no response.

"Mmm . . . Beast!"

The boy still didn't answer.

"Mmm . . . Murderer!"

Arlo was all of a sudden nervous. He started throwing names out, too. He had no idea what he was doing. But Arlo couldn't lose the boy now.

"Uh . . . Grubby!" Arlo said, trying to get the boy's attention.

The boy sniffed around in the dirt, ignoring them.

Arlo and Forrest continued to blurt out names, but nothing seemed to stick.

"Funeral Planner!"

"Cooty!"

"Hemorrhoid!"

"Squirt!"

"Fffffrank!"

"Stinky!"

"Manic!"

"Funky!"

"Violet!"

"Spike!"

"Lunatic!"

Finally, Arlo cried out, "Spot!"

The boy stopped, turned, and looked up. A big smile grew across Arlo's face. "C-come here, Spot! Come here!"

The boy happily trotted over to Arlo, and Forrest sighed. "He is named. You clearly are connected. . . . Good for you. On your path to Clawtooth Mountain, that creature will keep you safe. Don't ever lose him."

Then the red bird began to chirp loudly and angrily. "No. No . . . no! You—you can't have him, Debbie!" Forrest scolded the bird. She took off and flew at Arlo, chirping wildly, scaring him. Spot jumped at her, growling. Then the two ran as the bird continued to follow.

"Debbie!" They heard Forrest call. "Stop! You're better than this!"

Arlo and Spot hid behind a boulder to escape. As Debbie flew by with Forrest chasing behind her, the two unlikely friends looked at each other and laughed.

11

After the strange experience with Forrest, things changed between Spot and Arlo. Now they walked side by side. Instead of scowling and feeling angry at Spot, Arlo began to like the little guy. Spot helped Arlo forget about feeling afraid, even if just for a little while. The wilderness was less scary with Spot around . . . and a lot more fun.

Arlo watched Spot as he stopped to sniff an insect wing on the ground, investigating it. Spot followed the scent, sniffing along the ground and winding through the wilderness with Arlo following behind. Finally, Spot stopped, quivering as he thumped his leg against the ground in excitement. He led Arlo toward a bush, then grunted as he lifted up a giant leaf. Beneath it was a big, beautiful bug! Arlo smiled, checking out the bug's amazing eyes and incredible colors. Then Spot tore it apart! Arlo cringed, watching through squinted eyes as Spot ripped his meal to pieces.

Later, Arlo stepped on something small and hard, and crushed it with his weight. He lifted his foot and saw a delicious-looking nut split in half. Spot sniffed the ground curiously. Figuring Spot could find more, Arlo let him smell his foot. Just as Arlo had hoped, Spot set out, sniffing along the ground in search of more nuts.

As they approached a tree, Spot's leg started to shake against the ground and his whole body trembled with excitement. Arlo looked up. Spot had found them! There were dozens of nuts hanging from the branches of the tree. Arlo took some down and began to chew. They tasted a little funny, but he swallowed them down. Then he leaned in and took a closer look at the nuts in the tree. One of them moved! They weren't nuts—they were BUGS! And the tree was home to a whole colony! Gagging, Arlo tried to spit them out. But the colony was already bothered, and they started to swarm. Arlo was terrified and could do nothing but run away! Spot followed, and the two ran until they couldn't hear the buzzing behind them anymore. When they finally stopped, all Arlo and Spot could do was laugh.

SQUEAK!

A strange, high-pitched noise startled Arlo. He looked down and saw a gopher peeking its furry head out of a hole in the ground. Surprised, Arlo backed away. A second gopher popped up. *SQUEAK!* Spot tried to pounce on it, but it quickly ducked back down into its hole.

Spot smiled, and then he put his mouth over one of the holes and blew. The force of his breath caused a gopher to fly up into the air! When it fell down to the ground, it slipped back into its hole. Arlo laughed and joined in the fun, blowing and watching

The wilderness is a rugged and unpredictable place.
Despite its beauty, this environment is incredibly dangerous.

Three dinosaur eggs will soon hatch.
The biggest egg holds the smallest dinosaur. His name is Arlo.

Arlo is the only one who hasn't yet made his mark
on the family's silo.

Poppa shows Arlo a night sky filled with fireflies to teach him that
the world is more beautiful than scary.

Poppa shows Arlo how to set a trap to catch
the critter who's been stealing their food!

Arlo is a gentle soul. He wants to be brave and strong like Poppa,
but he's nervous about his new chore.

The trap works, and the critter is finally caught.
But Arlo doesn't have it in him to harm a living thing.

Arlo falls into the raging river. He gasps for air.
The current is too strong, and it carries him away.

In the darkness, Clawtooth Mountain looks like a monster's teeth, and the river is wilder and more dangerous than ever.

Out in the wilderness, Arlo and the critter meet. The two realize that they need each other if they're going to survive.

Arlo names the critter Spot. They use sticks to explain where they come from. Even though they have each other, they miss home.

On their journey, Arlo and Spot meet some T. rex ranchers. Arlo is caught in a longhorn stampede!

After a long day's work, Butch, Nash, Ramsey, and Arlo tell stories around the campfire. The T. rexes share some of their awesome adventures!

The friends peek through the clouds and watch the sunset together. It's incredible!

Arlo is filled with hope at the sight of Clawtooth Mountain.
Home isn't that far away!

Arlo follows the river and sees the family farm in the distance.
His long journey is almost over.

another gopher fly up. The two friends laughed as they orchestrated the airborne gophers.

The gophers were not pleased with being disturbed, and in frustration, one turned and bit Arlo. He and Spot were so surprised, they ran for safety and found themselves on a ledge above the river. From there, Arlo and Spot turned and watched as the gophers slowly and mysteriously sank back into the earth. Arlo was just about to climb toward solid ground, when, out of nowhere, one of the gophers popped back out and bit him. Then it quickly dropped back down into its hole. This shocked Arlo so much that he slipped, losing his footing and falling into the river below.

Panicking and gasping for air, Arlo struggled to keep his head above water. Spot jumped in after him and swam around, paddling his arms and kicking his legs. He continued to circle Arlo, as if trying to teach him how to swim. Arlo tried to imitate him, paddling and kicking his way through the water. It was difficult for the big dinosaur at first, but slowly he got the hang of it. Soon Arlo wasn't just keeping his head above water, he was swimming! Once he got a little more comfortable with his underwater moves, he followed Spot swiftly to shore.

Spot jumped out of the water, panting happily. Arlo proudly stepped out, then realized his body was covered in leeches! He screamed and ran, wiggling and flailing his body around, trying to shake off the blood-sucking worms. Once again, Arlo ran away shrieking. He had to dance for quite a while to shake them off. Luckily, Spot was there to help peel off the ones that wouldn't let go!

Later on, Arlo and Spot came upon some pieces of fruit scattered across the ground. Arlo ate as much as he could, then offered some to Spot. Laughing, the two stuffed their faces. It had been a long day. But after a while, they started to feel a little funny. Arlo looked at Spot, whose face had started to grow in all kinds of crazy ways. Spot looked at Arlo, who suddenly had five eyes! Something strange must have been in that fruit. They laughed and laughed.

In fact, it almost felt like they would laugh forever. But eventually they grew tired. And with their bellies pleasantly full, they finally fell asleep on the ground.

They woke up as night fell. Arlo and Spot walked through a meadow. Arlo saw a firefly and had an idea. He was reminded of that night with Poppa, back in the fields of their farm. "Spot, watch this!" he said.

Arlo brushed his tail through the tall meadow grass and hundreds of fireflies floated up. Spot loved it! He chased them excitedly, jumping and snapping at the air, trying to catch each one he saw. Arlo joined him; there were so many to chase.

Then Spot caught one with his hands and showed it to Arlo. The dinosaur smiled and gently blew on

it, just like Poppa had. Spot and Arlo watched as the firefly lit up, glowing brightly inside Spot's hands. Then Spot released it, and the firefly opened its wings and rose up into the sky. They watched it flickering and flashing as it flew off and disappeared into the night.

Arlo's smile soon faded as he thought about Poppa and his family at home. "I miss my family," he said quietly.

Spot looked up at Arlo with his face twisted in a confused expression and tilted his head. He didn't seem to understand.

"Family," Arlo said, trying to think of a way to explain.

Arlo broke some sticks and made dinosaur shapes with them. "That's me," he said, placing it on the ground in front of Spot. He continued, placing each one down as he spoke. "There's Libby, and Buck, and Momma . . ." He placed the last one down. "And—and Poppa." He drew a big circle in the dirt around all the figures and said the word again: "Family."

Spot sniffed the figures curiously but still didn't

seem to understand. "That's okay," Arlo said, trying to hide his feelings of disappointment.

Arlo rested on the ground as Spot scurried off, rummaging through some nearby bushes. He returned with some twigs, broke them, and set them down. They looked like three human shapes. Then Spot drew a big circle around his stick figures.

"Yes," said Arlo, perking up. "That's your family."

Spot took two of the figures and laid them flat on the ground. He covered them with dirt and looked up at Arlo, sniffing sadly. Arlo understood what Spot was trying to say: his parents had died.

Arlo took the figure of Poppa and covered it with dirt, too. "I miss him," Arlo said.

Spot reached over and patted Arlo's leg, comforting him. Then he returned to his stick figures and howled at the moon. "Arroooowah!"

Even though Spot didn't talk, he had a way of communicating that he was sad. And that he was still hurting as he remembered painful things. Arlo had been hurting over Poppa for a long time. And until now, he'd never really tried to talk about it.

But this was as good a time as any. Arlo joined Spot and howled, too.

Under the giant sky and a million twinkling stars, the two friends howled at the moon, releasing their sadness into the night.

"Arrrrooooooooowah!"

12

The next morning Arlo woke to Spot running in his sleep, making growling noises, and pounding into Arlo's nose with his feet. The dinosaur snapped awake and lifted his head away from the barrage of toes and heels. Then Spot woke up; he looked up at Arlo with a big grin. Arlo smiled back.

It was time to start their day. They got up and began walking along the river. Almost out of nowhere, dark clouds appeared and instantly grew darker. The wind picked up and started blowing the leaves off the trees. Soon branches began cracking and whipping through the air. As the wind grew stronger, debris flew toward them, and Arlo started to panic.

BOOM!

The sound of thunder startled Arlo, causing him to flinch and shudder. He looked at Spot, ahead in the distance, and screamed to him. "We should stop!" But Spot couldn't hear him over the angry sounds of the sky.

The thunder roared even louder and lightning flashed as the storm intensified. It reminded Arlo of that day in the wilderness with Poppa. It was as if he could see himself and Poppa in the pass, the rushing water coming toward them, and that terrible feeling. . . . Arlo remembered Poppa screaming for him to run, right before the water took him away forever. The thought of it made Arlo feel even more frightened and he started to run, as if trying to escape the storm.

Spot saw Arlo and turned back to follow him.

Terrified, Arlo scrambled up a hill.

BOOM!

The deafening sound of the thunder, now right overhead, caused him to slip and fall down a muddy slope.

A large old tree, having been taken down by the wind, lay on its side. Its giant root ball had been ripped up from the ground and was big enough for Arlo to hide under. He ran to it and pressed his body against it, trying to shield himself from the maelstrom. Arlo stayed there, curled up and trembling, wishing for the storm to pass.

When the wind finally calmed and the sun's rays cracked through the clouds, the light revealed the devastation it had left in its wake. The wilderness looked completely different. Trees were knocked over, shelters destroyed, and debris was scattered everywhere. It was as if the wilderness had been turned inside out.

Spot, with his nose to the ground, sniffed around in search of Arlo. He dug through a pile of leaves and found him, still curled up under the giant root ball. The dinosaur stumbled forward and looked around, panicking at the sight of the wilderness.

"Wh-where's the river?" Arlo asked, whipping his head around nervously. "I've lost the river!" Frenzied,

Arlo ran, looking every which way, searching for signs that would lead him home.

Then a shadow passed overhead, blocking out the sun. Arlo looked up and saw a group of Pterodactyls, giant winged reptiles, flying in formation like a search-and-rescue team. It seemed that they were looking for signs of life in the wreckage below. Arlo was overjoyed to see them and figured they could help him get home. He urgently called up to them, waving his arms. "Help!"

But as soon as Spot saw the Pterodactyls, he scurried off to hide.

Three Pterodactyls touched ground in front of Arlo as the others continued on their way.

"You wounded, friend?" asked one.

"No, I'm not hurt," answered Arlo.

The first Pterodactyl turned to the other two. "Coldfront. Downpour. Search for others." The two headed off and went through the rubble, searching.

"Wait, I'm lost," said Arlo. "I need to get home, to Clawtooth Mountain."

"Mountain range with three points?" he asked

"Yes!" Arlo said, thrilled that he had heard of it.

"I've been there," he said. "But spit, kid, you're not even close. Still I know the way."

Relieved, the young dinosaur smiled and introduced himself, "My name is Arlo."

"I used to have a name like that once, but that was before I found the storm. The storm swept me up . . . and I was afraid for my life. But the storm gave me a relevation, and I wasn't scared anymore," he said.

"Relevation?" Arlo asked.

"Yeah, Re-LE-VA-tion!" the Pterodactyl repeated. "I was at a real low point, you know, and the storm swept me up in a . . . real high point and then left me at a higher RELEVATION."

As he talked, the Pterodactyl raised his wings high and waved them back and forth.

"Wow," Arlo said.

"That's when the storm gave me my new name," he explained. Then he turned to one of the other Pterodactyls. "Because what do we say?" he asked.

"Oh yeah, the storm provides," Downpour repeated.

The spooky Pterodactyl finally introduced himself to Arlo. "You can call me Thunderclap," he said.

"Can you help me get home?" asked Arlo. He was starting to feel a little uncomfortable.

"Oh yeah, you betcha," said Thunderclap, looking around.

Then the other Pterodactyl, Coldfront, called out, "I found someone! Over here!" He tried to lift up a heavy, cracked log, and Downpour flew over to help.

A little critter stuck his paw out from the rubble, scratching and clawing, trying to get out.

"You know, we could use your help over here," Thunderclap said to Arlo.

Arlo nodded and walked over to them. The three Pterodactyls lifted one end of the cracked log while Arlo whipped his tail against it like an axe, whacking it until it split in half.

"Wahoo!" The Pterodactyls hooted and hollered with excitement, letting the other end of the log drop to the ground. They landed, pushed aside the rest of the debris, and then Thunderclap reached into the rubble and picked up the furry little creature.

"It's a critter," said Arlo.

"Now a freed critter, thanks to you," Thunderclap said. He lifted it high and looked as if he were going to put it on the ground. But instead of releasing it, he threw back his head and dropped it into his long beak. He ate it!

Arlo was horrified. He looked around and saw Spot hiding under some debris. He was shaking, and Arlo could tell he was terrified. He had never seen Spot look so scared.

Thunderclap had clearly enjoyed his food. "You know, I just want to take a moment and thank the storm for this meal," he said.

But then Downpour and Coldfront snapped at the foxtail hanging out of Thunderclap's mouth. Thunderclap quickly whirled at the other Pterodactyls, and soon, all three were fighting and growling. But it was clear that Thunderclap was the most vicious.

"I've seen the eye of the storm, and I forgot what fear is . . . I'm not afraid of nothing," he warned—his crazy eyes darting all over the place. Arlo slowly started to back up, toward the place where Spot was hiding. Then Thunderclap flew over, cutting him off. Arlo gasped. "Where you goin', friend?" asked Thunderclap, menacingly.

Downpour and Coldfront landed behind Arlo. He was surrounded. Trapped.

"I-I'm—I need to get home," Arlo stammered.

"And I said we would get you home," said Thunderclap. He touched Arlo's shoulder and began to sniff the air. "Friend, you have a critter of your own."

Coldfront sniffed around, searching, too. "I smell it. One of the juicy ones," he added.

"Where is it?" screeched Downpour.

The towering Pterodactyls stared down Arlo, waiting for an answer. Arlo pointed in the opposite direction of where Spot was hiding. "Over there, by that leaning tree."

Downpour and Coldfront went over to the tree,

using their claws and beaks to wildly scratch and scrape around the rubble, searching for Spot. But Thunderclap stayed behind, watching Arlo and staring deep into his eyes. Arlo accidentally gave Spot a worried glance, and Thunderclap immediately knew where the boy was hiding.

"The storm provides," Thunderclap said matter-of-factly and flew over to Spot's hiding place.

"No!" Arlo yelled. Spot quickly scrambled, slipping right beneath Thunderclap's claws, and took off running. Thunderclap flapped his wings and flew, chasing Spot from above. Arlo dashed toward them, scooped Spot up, and bolted as the Pterodactyls continued their pursuit.

Spot hopped on top of Arlo's back and held on tight as Arlo raced as fast as he could. Arlo saw a big, long-neck dinosaur grazing and yelled to it. "Oh . . . help!"

He ran toward it with the Pterodactyls right behind him. When he got close enough, he saw it wasn't a big, long-neck dinosaur at all—it was two dinosaurs—and they were T. rexes!

13

Arlo screamed as the ferocious T. rexes came roaring toward them. He turned to try and run the other way, but the Pterodactyls were blocking him. With nowhere to go and no idea what to do, Arlo curled up into a ball over Spot, protecting him.

The T. rexes were closing in, roaring so loudly it made Arlo shiver. But instead of attacking Spot and Arlo, the T. rexes grabbed the Pterodactyls with their teeth and flung them from side to side! After a few seconds of fighting, the Pterodactyls were scared off and flapped toward the horizon. Then the T. rexes turned and set their sights on Spot and Arlo.

Arlo, frozen with fear, could barely breathe as the T. rexes stomped toward him and Spot. One of them leaned right above Arlo, who was scared to death as he looked up at the T. rex's enormous toothy mouth. Arlo flinched, closing his eyes tightly as he prepared to be eaten. But the T. rex put out her arm and helped him up.

"I hate those kind," she said. "Lyin' sons of crawdads. Pickin' on a kid!"

Spot smiled up at her, panting, with his tongue hanging out and leaned against her leg. She put her hand down for Spot to sniff and scratched the top of his head. "Well, ain't you the cutest thing," she said, adoringly.

Arlo smiled. "Hmmm, he likes you."

"Imagine that, Ramsey!" said the other T. rex, laughing and getting right in front of her. "Even with your stinky face."

Ramsey snapped at him, annoyed. "Nash! Boundaries!" She used her arms to demonstrate. "This is my personal bubble."

"Naw," Nash said. "That ain't your bubble. This is your bubble." Nash climbed on her, and they started wrestling, punching, and kicking each other.

An even *bigger* T. rex angrily stomped over to them. "Nash!" he scolded. "Get out of your sister's bubble." Ramsey and Nash looked up at their father, Butch, and stopped wrestling. Once Butch turned toward Arlo, Nash gave Ramsey one last push.

Arlo looked up at Butch. The big T. rex towered over him. Arlo noticed an ugly scar across his giant face. He was an incredibly scary looking dinosaur! Butch eyed Arlo intensely, looking him up and down. "You got no business being out here," Butch said.

"Yes, sir, I don't. I'm trying to get home, but I lost the river. Please, my Momma needs me," Arlo pleaded.

Arlo asked if they knew the way to Clawtooth Mountain, but the T. rexes didn't have time to help. They were looking for their herd of longhorns and needed to find them right away.

"My genius brother lost our whole herd in one day," Ramsey explained.

"I did not lose them, Ramsey!" shouted Nash defensively. "How many times do I have to tell you this? They just, um . . . they just wandered off!"

"And we still gotta find 'em," said Butch. "We can't help ya kid." Butch started to move off, but Arlo stopped him. He offered the T. rexes a deal. He and Spot would help them find the herd if the T. rexes could take them toward Clawtooth Mountain.

"Spot can sniff out anything!" Arlo offered, trying to convince Butch to accept his offer. Butch thought about it for a moment and then agreed.

"Come on, Spot. Sniff it out, boy," Arlo said. Ramsey held out a piece of longhorn fur for Spot to smell so he could get the scent and track the herd. Spot immediately took off, sniffing and hunting.

"Good boy, Spot!" cheered Arlo. But Butch wasn't so sure this would work.

The T. rexes slowly followed Spot and Arlo while Spot continued, nose to the ground, sniffing in search of the longhorns.

"If you're pullin' my leg, I'm gonna eat yours,"

Butch said, frustrated and impatient.

Arlo chuckled nervously and whispered to Spot to try and move a little faster. Spot picked up the pace, searching through the open range.

Moments later, Spot shivered and tapped his leg against the ground, thumping it with excitement. Arlo happily blurted, "He's got something!"

The T. rexes anxiously ran forward. Then Spot lunged at the ground and snatched a bug. He gobbled it down, growling and chewing as Arlo nervously smiled.

"Ah, dang," said Ramsey, disappointed.

Butch frowned as he circled back to Arlo. "That leg is looking pretty good about now," he said.

Suddenly, Spot began to race around, barking excitedly.

"He found somethin'!" said Ramsey.

They followed Spot and saw a single longhorn's track leading through some tall reeds. Beyond the reeds were dozens of tracks!

"Whooooeee!" cried Nash. "We got 'em!"

"Wait," said Arlo, noticing a bright blue feather on the ground. "Do longhorns have feathers?"

"Rustlers," muttered Butch with a disgusted scowl. He realized that thieves must have taken the herd!

14

Arlo gulped. "Rustlers?" he asked.

Butch walked ahead and found a dead longhorn in the tumbleweed. "We gotta move," said Butch. "Hya!"

The T. rexes took off, running swiftly and quietly. Spot and Arlo followed as they tracked the prints until the prints disappeared over the top of a small hill. When they got closer to the edge, the T. rexes crawled on their bellies to get a view of the herd a short distance away. The dinosaurs quietly watched the scene below.

Arlo crouched down, too. There—below the big

blue sky—was the herd, quietly grazing in the tall grass. It seemed very peaceful.

"I don't see any rustlers," whispered Arlo, wondering where the thieves could be.

"They're out there," said Butch, inching forward. He turned to Arlo and squinted, sizing him up. "I got a job for you."

"I'm not really good at . . . *jobs,*" Arlo responded timidly.

Butch pointed out to the right of the herd. "I need you to keep on the dodge and sidle up the lob lolly past them hornheads, just hootin' and hollerin' to score off them rustlers. We'll cut dirt and get the bulge on 'em."

"What?" Arlo asked, blank-faced.

"He just wants you to get on that rock and scream," Ramsey said, clarifying. She pointed to a large rock in the field near the longhorns.

"They'll come right at you," added Butch. "You hold your ground. Don't move."

"Don't move?" asked Arlo nervously. "What if

they have claws and big teeth?"

"Don't overthink it," Butch said. Then he pushed Arlo right out into the field!

With Spot on his back, Arlo nervously looked around. He glanced at the T. rexes, and Butch nodded, encouraging Arlo to go on.

Arlo took a deep breath and tried to get over his fear. He moved slowly, creeping through the grass. When he turned back, the T. rexes were gone! He panted as he anxiously continued toward the large rock.

Once he reached it, he carefully climbed up to the top. Trembling, his legs shook and his knees knocked into each other as he tried to muster up some courage. He took another deep breath and, finally, opened his mouth to roar. A low, strained whimper came out. Spot watched as he tried again. But Arlo's "roar" came out like a strangled whisper.

Taking matters into his own hands, Spot chomped down on Arlo's leg and Arlo let out a piercing scream!

In an instant, Arlo saw the tall grass quiver and move. He could hear something coming toward them rapidly, but he couldn't see what it was. His mouth went dry and he could barely breathe. Once again, Arlo was terrified.

Three of the thieves appeared: they were nasty-looking Raptors. Each had a mouth full of big pointy teeth and a sharp, curved talon on each foot. Arlo turned to see another one—even bigger than the others—coming right at him. He froze in fear.

"What are you up to, boy?" asked one.

"N-n-n-nothing," Arlo said.

The female Raptor cackled. "Nothin'? What's your name?" she asked.

"Uh . . . Ah-ah-Arl-Arlo."

"Well, ah-ah-ah-Arlo, you don't look like you're doin' nothing. What's he look like he's doing to you, Lurleane?" asked the big Raptor.

"Oh, come on, Bubbha, ask me! Ask me what I think they're doin'," said the other male Raptor.

"Pervis, shut your mouth!" Bubbha said.

"Looks like he's trespassin'," Lurleane snarled.

"And what do we do with trespassers? Tell 'em,

Earl," Bubbha said with a growl.

"We kill 'em!" Earl exclaimed.

In an instant, Earl lunged at Arlo. Arlo closed his eyes, sure he was a goner. But then Butch leaped out of the grass and grabbed the Raptor midair! The other Raptors jumped and bounced, and Nash swiped at them. The Raptors and T. rexes battled. Arlo was right in the middle of the chaotic brawl!

Pervis landed on a rock in front of Arlo and jumped at him. "I GOT YA!" he yelled, standing right over Arlo.

BOOM!

Butch head-butted Pervis and he went flying. Pervis landed with a thud, right in the middle of the herd. The noise stirred the longhorns up and they began to stampede. They trampled right over Pervis and were headed toward Arlo.

Arlo was petrified, but Spot barked and hopped onto his back, snapping him out of it. Arlo took off running.

Ramsey dashed toward the stampede and called to

her brother. "Nash! The herd! Hya!"

"Giddyup! Come on now! Giddyup! Hya!" Nash shouted, following close behind.

Then Ramsey noticed a Raptor right behind Nash. "Watch out!" she screamed.

The giant Raptor jumped onto Nash and they began to fight. Nash got in a few good punches, but Bubbha managed to peg him down. Bubbha held up his claws, ready to strike, when Ramsey charged into the fight—nailing him with an impressive tail whip. *THUMP!*

The Raptor went flying.

Meanwhile, Arlo ran from the stampeding herd, getting tossed around along the way. Spot barked as Arlo ran behind a boulder. Arlo caught his breath, but Spot continued to bark and growl.

Just then, Lurleane landed on a nearby boulder. Arlo ducked for cover, trying to stay hidden. She sniffed around, looking for someone to fight. All of a sudden, Spot jumped out, growling at her and egging her on. But Arlo grabbed him back, hoping she wouldn't find them.

"Come on out—Momma wants to play with you," Lurleane said creepily. "I know you're there. I can SMELL ya."

Without warning, Butch charged in with Pervis on his back, and Lurleane joined in the attack on Butch. Arlo tried to get out of the way, but he got whacked by Butch's tail in the scuffle.

The Raptors pinned Butch to the ground right in front of Arlo. "Nab his tail!" Butch yelled, but Arlo was scared stiff. Spot nudged him, growling, and Arlo knew he had to help. Without giving it another thought, Arlo ran straight at Pervis, screaming like a crazed dinosaur.

Arlo head-butted the Raptor clear across the field! He couldn't believe he had actually done it. He smiled proudly, but the feeling quickly faded as soon as Lurleane slinked toward him.

"I'm going to love ending you," she said with a terrible growl. She lunged at Arlo. But before she could reach him, Butch snatched her up by the tail.

Butch roared as he hurled her off into the distance. Then he chased the other Raptors away, biting their blue-feathered tails as they ran.

It had been quite a battle, and the T. rexes celebrated their victory with a hearty roar. Then Ramsey looked over to Arlo and nudged him. It was obvious that she wanted Arlo to roar, too! After all, Arlo had helped defeat them. He let out the loudest roar he could muster.

Nash ran up. "Come on, we gotta drive this herd outta here," he said, nipping at one of the longhorns. "Hya! Come on now!"

Arlo and Spot couldn't believe it, but they'd survived. They shared a glance and proudly tagged along with the T. rexes and the herd as they moved the longhorns on to safer pastures.

The friends galloped with the T. rexes into the sunset. Even though they were exhausted, they breathed a sigh of relief.

For the first time in a long time, Arlo had reasons to be confident. He'd finished a job. He'd survived.

He'd participated in the rescue of the longhorns in a big way. Loping across the plains, he couldn't help but think that he'd be home soon.

He could feel it.

15

As the big moon glowed above, Arlo, Spot, Nash, Ramsey, and Butch sat around a crackling campfire. Nash blew a tune on a bug harmonica while Ramsey played with Spot.

She held a stick while Spot chased it around and tugged on it, growling and loving every second. Ramsey pulled back on the stick, and Spot held on so tightly that when she raised the stick up, he was hoisted into the air. Then he started chewing on her arm. "Aren't you the cutest?" Ramsey said, chuckling.

"You and that critter showed real grit today," Butch said.

Arlo couldn't help but smile.

Nash stopped playing the harmonica and held it up. He asked Arlo if he would trade Spot for it.

"Thanks, but Spot ain't for tradin'," said Arlo.

"Your loss," said Nash. Then he tossed the bug into his mouth and ate it.

Arlo's forearm throbbed with pain. He touched the small bruise and cut, checking out its severity. Ramsey took a look at it and gently said, "That's a good one. Gonna scar up real good."

"That's nothing!" said Nash. "Look at this!" he lifted his foot and held up his leg, showing off an ugly scar on his calf. "I run into fifteen outlaw Steggos," he said, getting into the story. "They were all bigger 'n me. An' meaner than me."

"What happened?" Arlo asked, intrigued.

"Fought 'em off, of course! Was winnin', too. Then one gets his dang spiky tail stuck in my foot and pulls."

"Whoa." Arlo was impressed.

Nash put his foot right into the campfire. "Still can't feel my toes," he said, holding his foot over the dancing flames and wiggling his toes.

Then Ramsey shared a story. "Once, a stampede of longhorns was comin' right at me. But my tail was stuck between a rock and a hard place. I was dead for sure." She whipped her tail around, revealing a short nub. "So I chewed the dang thing off!" She and Nash howled with laughter.

"Who does that? Nobody does that," Nash said through his laughter.

Arlo stared at Ramsey's chewed tail in shock. It was still long enough to use, but the end looked knobby, crooked, and downright disgusting. She held it up, close to his face, and he pretended to laugh along with them. But then he pushed her tail aside with an uncomfortable chuckle.

Arlo turned to Butch and asked him how he'd gotten his scar.

"I don't know if you're ready for that story," said Butch ominously.

"I can take it," answered Arlo.

Nash and Ramsey excitedly asked Butch to tell

the story. It was one of their favorites. "That's a good one!" said Ramsey.

Butch turned his head to show off the *huge* scar along the side of his face. It looked even meaner in the firelight. Butch cleared his throat and began telling his tale.

"It was a hundred degrees in the shade. I walked for five days with no water. Then I saw it. A pretty pond. I bent down to take a drink, when these crocs launched outta the water! One croc bit me on the face. Ain't no way I wasn't its supper, except for one thing—I wasn't ready for dyin' that day. I bit one croc in half, tail-whipped the other, and the last one, well . . ." Butch paused dramatically as his eyes went wide. "I drowned that croc in my own blood."

"Whoa," Arlo said.

"*Dang!*" Ramsey and Nash sang.

"Look, look," said Nash, holding up his arm. "Gives me lil' goosies every time."

"I love that story," added Ramsey. "Show him your souvenir!"

Butch pulled back his cheek to show off a crocodile tooth lodged in his jaw! He wiggled it back and forth with his tongue, like a loose tooth. Arlo went pale at the sight of it.

Ramsey leaned over to Arlo and whispered, "Ain't that just too good?"

Arlo nodded in awe.

Nash leaned toward Butch. "Can I touch it this time?"

"No," said Butch, quickly.

"You guys would've liked my Poppa," Arlo said. "He wasn't scared of anything." He sighed, thinking about Poppa. Butch watched Arlo's face, as if reading his thoughts. "I'm done being scared," Arlo added.

"Who said I'm not scared?" asked Butch.

Arlo looked at him with surprise. "But you took on a croc—"

"And I was scared doing it. If you ain't scared of a croc bitin' ya on the face, you ain't alive," Butch said.

Arlo had never thought about it that way.

"You can't get rid of fear. It's like Mother Nature.

You can't beat her or outrun her. But you can get through it. You can find out what you're made of."

Arlo gazed at Butch as he took in his words, thinking about what he had said. Then something drifted down from the sky and fell right in front of Arlo. It immediately snapped him out of his thoughts. He focused and saw more floating down. "The first snow," said Arlo somberly.

"It's early this year," said Ramsey.

"And I gotta get home to Momma," Arlo said definitively. He was worried about his family. He knew that once the snow started, the farm and their supplies had to be ready in order to make it through the winter.

"A deal's a deal," said Butch. "At first light, we ride."

16

As the sun broke over the horizon, the light dusting of snow sparkled against the ground. Ever faithful, the T. rexes herded the longhorns on.

Arlo and Spot followed, helping to drive the herd from behind. When Butch noticed the herd splitting off on one side, he called to Arlo for help. "Hey, kid, head 'em off before those longhorns split!"

Arlo looked back at Spot and confidently nodded. Then the two of them ran ahead of the longhorns that were breaking away and stood directly in their path. The longhorns raced toward them at full speed. But the brave friends held their ground as the longhorns closed the gap between them. Arlo whipped his tail against the ground, whacking it again and again. He even roared at them, forcing the longhorns to head the other way. It worked! The longhorns were so startled that they joined the rest of the herd and were back on track.

Arlo and Spot continued to chase them, making sure they stayed with the main herd. Spot panted with excitement and Arlo smiled. It felt good to help and be part of a team.

Butch passed by, giving them a chuckle and a nod as he ran. He was impressed.

Once they made it over a slope and through the distant ridges, Arlo could make out the snowcapped peaks of Clawtooth Mountain. He felt a rush of excitement. "There's home!" he exclaimed.

"Whooeee!" yelped Nash.

"Wahoo!" shouted Ramsey.

The T. rexes had to move and drive the herd down south, so it was time to say good-bye.

"You hurry on back to your momma, and don't

stop for nothin'," said Ramsey.

Arlo thanked them. "I sure appreciate you lookin' out for me," he added.

But before Arlo and Spot headed toward the pass, Butch gave Arlo some parting words. "You'll be all right. You're one tough kid."

Arlo smiled. That meant a lot coming from Butch. The T. rexes continued on with the herd, while Arlo and Spot headed toward the pass.

As Arlo and Spot continued their journey alongside the river, Arlo felt like he was walking on air. Knowing he was close to home made him feel happy. He got a surge of energy and excitement. He and Spot began running and jumping, playing and laughing on their way.

Arlo saw a flock of wild birds pecking around in the distance and ran toward them. Spot jumped up on Arlo's back and climbed to the top of his head. Spot's tongue hung out happily and waved in the wind as they galloped toward the flock, picking up speed. Once they reached them, the birds scattered, flapping their wings and taking to the sky.

Spot howled with delight. "Arooowah!"

Arlo joined in, howling back at him as he jumped over boulders and swerved past trees.

Eventually they reached a rocky hill, and Arlo continued to jump across the rough terrain. He tossed Spot way up into the clouds, and Spot caught a glimpse of the sun. Arlo laughed as Spot cheered; he was loving every minute. He signaled to Arlo to toss him up again and again.

When they got to the top, Spot sat on Arlo's head and the two peeked through the clouds. They watched the sunset together. It was spectacular.

"Wow," said Arlo. The friends looked at each other and smiled, sharing a moment of complete joy.

17

The next day, as Spot and Arlo continued, they heard the low rumble of thunder in the distance. They could see the river and Clawtooth Mountain just up around the bend. "It's so close," said Arlo. "We're almost there, Spot!" Arlo yelled with excitement, and Spot joined in with a howl. After so much action, it felt great to laugh and howl together—just for fun.

But then . . .

"Arrooowah!"

Someone howled back!

Spot began looking around for the source of the noise. Almost immediately, he and Arlo saw a human figure on the ridge ahead.

Intrigued, Spot jumped down from Arlo's back and began to investigate. Arlo watched as Spot moved away from him, approaching the human. The possibility that Spot could leave him crept into Arlo's thoughts and made him extremely uncomfortable. He and Spot had been through a lot together, and Arlo liked having him around. The idea of being without Spot was just too much for Arlo to take. So when the human started to move down the ridge, Arlo quickly scooped Spot up and put him on his back. "We need to get home," Arlo said, moving back toward the river.

Arlo and Spot moved off the trail and above the tree line, heading up the river. Soon the wind started whipping through the trees, and the sounds of thunder came closer. The storm was picking up.

Drip.

Drip.

Arlo eyed the sky, feeling the drops of rain. The big gray storm clouds seemed to swell before his eyes. Lightning pulsed all around him and, as the rain poured down, Arlo's feet began to sink into the soft mud. Once again, he was reminded of the day he had been in the wilderness with Poppa. All of Arlo's terrible fears rushed back to him and he began to crumble. "I can't," he said, panicking.

He tried to get his bearings and looked up for some kind of help. Instead, he saw what looked like a shark fin cutting through the storm clouds. First there was one, then another, and another . . . they were circling—just like sharks about to attack.

Another flash of lightning lit up the sky, and Arlo could see that the shark fins were actually large wings—the Pterodactyls were back.

They laughed and hissed cruelly as Arlo panicked. The dinosaur lost sight of them for a second, but before he could think of what to do next, they swooped down, diving and beating Arlo, their talons and wings in his face. The Pterodactyls scratched and pecked, forcing him up a ridge. Arlo screamed, running backward as they attacked, pushing him to the very edge! With nowhere to run, Arlo stood as the Pterodactyls continued to strike, scratching him and beating his face with their giant wings. Spot growled and barked defensively, trying to protect Arlo.

Whoosh!

Thunderclap swooped down and picked up Spot in his talons! Arlo grabbed onto Spot, too. The enemies struggled, tugging Spot in both directions.

"No!" Arlo screamed through clenched teeth. Spot reached for Arlo, but couldn't get to him. "Spot! Spot!" Arlo cried as he lost his grip. But it was no use. Arlo gasped as Thunderclap carried Spot away.

The other Pterodactyls turned their attention to Arlo. He dodged and ducked, but the ground below him was squishy and soft from the fresh rain. Arlo tried to stay standing, but he lost his footing and slid off the ridge. He landed in the sharp, tangled brambles below. He tried to wrestle his way out, but every time he moved, the brambles seemed to tighten around him. He was stuck.

The Pterodactyls tried to get to him, but they

weren't able to get through the thick, thorny shrub.

Finally, the Pterodactyls gave up on Arlo and headed toward Thunderclap and Spot. Arlo struggled, trying to keep his eyes on Spot and yelling his name. But the brambles held him back, tightening around him like thorny chains. A large bramble was tangled around his neck, and Arlo watched helplessly as the Pterodactyls took Spot away, disappearing into the storm clouds.

Thunder boomed as the storm continued to get worse. Arlo gave one last pull at the brambles. A big piece of rock came loose, hitting him on the head. Everything went black.

18

When Arlo eventually opened his eyes, he could see something large moving toward him. But he couldn't quite make out what it was.

Crack!

Crack!

Something was chopping the brambles in half, loosening their grip on Arlo. A flood of emotion washed over him. It was Poppa! He was standing right there! Arlo was shocked.

Poppa continued to pull the brambles off, freeing him completely. "C'mon, Arlo, we gotta move," Poppa said.

Arlo stood up. He was entirely confused. "You're alive?" he asked.

"Storm's gettin' worse," he said. "Let's get you home."

Arlo looked at Poppa uncertainly—was it true? Was it really him?

Poppa smiled and curled his tail around Arlo, hugging him. He led Arlo out of the brambles.

Boom.

Boom.

Crack!

The storm continued to rage angrily. Arlo looked up. "My friend, Spot—" he said, slowing down. "He helped me, and now he's in trouble."

But Poppa kept walking.

As the thunder roared and debris flew, Arlo flinched. He was scared and leaned into Poppa, just like he used to.

But after everything that Spot and Arlo had been through together, Arlo knew he couldn't leave him behind. "Poppa, we have to go back," he said.

But Poppa didn't respond.

"Poppa!" Arlo yelled. "Stop!"

Arlo was frustrated. Then he looked down and realized that Poppa wasn't leaving any footprints. Arlo slowed down and eventually stopped. Poppa's tail slid from around him.

He looked up at his father and asked, "You're not really here, are you?"

Poppa finally turned around. His face was full of concern. "It's okay," he said.

"I'm still scared," Arlo admitted. "But Spot needs me, so I gotta go help him. Because I love him."

"I knew you had it in you," Poppa said proudly. "Go take care of that critter."

Poppa then faded into the rain.

Arlo opened his eyes. He was still caged in a tangle of brambles. Poppa had only been a dream.

But Arlo felt different . . . he felt determined. As the rain poured down, he strained to break free—

Snap!

Snap!

The brambles were breaking.

Snap!

He continued to work at them.

Snap!

He broke them one section at a time. One after another.

Snap!

Snap!

Snap!

He pushed through and got himself out. Then he ran off to find Spot.

19

The storm raged as Arlo ran up the mountain as fast as he could. He began to howl, calling for Spot. A bolt of lightning struck the ground and hit a nearby tree. Arlo dodged out of the way as the giant tree crashed to the wilderness floor with a deafening boom.

Arlo continued to howl until, finally, he heard Spot howl back. Arlo followed the sounds of Spot's howling until he found five Pterodactyls at the river—huddling around a dead, hollow tree. Spot was ducked down, inside the tree. He was hurt and trying to protect himself.

The Pterodactyls growled and hissed at Spot,

smashing into the tree over and over again. They knocked it back and forth, tossing Spot around inside. Arlo could hear them arguing over who would get to him first.

Arlo couldn't take it. He raced down the steep slope, charging at the Pterodactyls. Surprising everyone—even himself—Arlo head-butted one of them right into the river!

"Well, look who got relevated," Thunderclap mused. Arlo charged at them again. This time at full speed. Thunderclap flew toward Arlo and dodged just as he was about to hit him, causing Arlo to slip in the mud. Thunderclap laughed wickedly.

The Pterodactyls flew at Arlo, snapping at him and beating him with their wings. They worked together to lift him into the air. Trapped, Spot cried from the tree, pained at not being able to help his friend. Then Thunderclap left Arlo and headed straight for Spot.

"Spot!" Arlo called.

Thunderclap growled menacingly as he closed in on Spot.

Arlo sensed the ground tremble and looked upriver. He gasped. Something was coming toward them. Arlo tried to fight off the Pterodactyls but couldn't manage to get away. They still had him off the ground.

Thunderclap growled as he clawed at Spot, forcing him to go deeper into the tree.

The Pterodactyls cackled, teasing and pulling Arlo in midair. Then Arlo noticed a nearby tree. Using all his strength, he whacked his tail into it, just like he had when herding the longhorns, and snapped the tree in half. The falling tree startled the Pterodactyls, and they lost their grip. They dropped Arlo, and the tree smashed right into them!

One of the other Pterodactyls growled angrily as it flew toward Arlo, ready to kill. Without missing a beat, Arlo uprooted another tree and launched it at the flying beast. The tree smacked right into the Pterodactyl and knocked it into the water.

Arlo looked over at Thunderclap, who was still attacking Spot. Arlo ran toward him, ready to fight. He roared so loudly that Thunderclap took one look at him, screamed, and flew off.

But there was no time to celebrate. All of a sudden, the ground beneath them shook. Arlo looked upriver again and could see the water crashing down the pass. A flash flood raged toward them.

The rapids began to push the tree where Spot was hiding farther into the water. Spot reached for Arlo. He tried with all his might but couldn't get to him. Arlo ran upriver to Spot, toward the rushing flood! The storm blew hard against him, but he continued, fighting his way toward his friend.

As debris rushed by and the river raged, it knocked down trees in its path. "Spot!" called Arlo, trying to outpace the flood.

Spot was scared. He hunkered down into the tree for protection. Arlo leaped between Spot and the wall of debris to protect him.

BAM!

The debris smashed into Arlo midair, and he was knocked into the rapids.

Screaming, Arlo struggled to swim against the

current. When he resurfaced, he searched frantically for Spot.

"Spot!" Arlo called, gasping for air. Finally, he saw him: Spot was unconscious, inside the dead tree. And the tree was sinking.

Arlo swam as fast as he could toward Spot, fighting the current and dodging flying debris along the way. The rushing sounds of a giant waterfall became louder and louder. Trees crashed and branches flew. Eventually Spot opened his eyes and saw Arlo swimming toward him.

A massive tree headed straight for Arlo with its spiky branches sticking out every which way. Arlo dove down, swimming beneath it. The sharp branches jutted out and scratched his skin, but he continued on. He needed to reach Spot. When Arlo came up for air, he was almost there. But the waterfall was approaching!

All of a sudden, Spot jumped out of the hollow tree. Arlo and Spot swam toward each other, trying to beat the rapids. Just as they found each other, Arlo curled around Spot, and they fell over the cliff and into the falls.

When they came up at the bottom, Arlo was holding Spot. He quickly got them both out of the water and checked to see if Spot was okay. Spot opened his eyes, and they looked at each other gratefully. Bruised and battered, they had made it. Exhausted, Arlo put his head down and breathed a deep sigh of relief.

20

The next morning brought clear skies and a renewed sense that everything was going to be okay. Spot rode on Arlo's back, and Arlo walked confidently, feeling proud that they had made it through the terrible storm. "We're home, Spot," Arlo said, relieved.

"Arrooowah!"

They heard a distant howl and turned to see a human man up on a hill. Then a mother and two children appeared—it was a family. Arlo slowly moved toward them. The father came forward and Spot hopped off Arlo's back to investigate.

The humans sniffed each other as Arlo watched.

The father tousled Spot's hair, and the rest of the family gathered affectionately around Spot.

Spot looked at Arlo and ran back toward him. He jumped up on Arlo's back, ready to keep going. But Arlo lowered him down and gently slid him off. Spot didn't understand. Then Arlo pushed him toward the family.

Spot still didn't understand. He ran back to Arlo. But Arlo, again, pushed him to the family. Then he drew a circle in the ground around all of them, just like he had with the stick figures on the night they howled at the moon. Spot and Arlo locked eyes. Spot understood.

The friends had tears in their eyes as they hugged. They both knew this was good-bye.

Once they parted, Arlo watched as Spot trotted toward the family. The father stuck out his hand to Spot, and the boy grabbed it, walking beside him, as if they had always been together. As the family turned, Spot looked back at Arlo one last time, sending up a howl. Arlo knew things were as they should be, but he felt a tightness in his throat as he howled back. He couldn't help but feel a little sad. He missed Spot already.

With a tear running down his cheek, Arlo stood and watched as his friend walked away.

21

The big, clear sky was bright blue as Arlo walked the last part of his journey alone. This time, he walked through the familiar mountain pass without fear. Regardless of whether the wilderness chose to hit him with another storm, he knew he would soon be home. He would make it.

Beyond the mountain pass, Arlo saw the farm. The fields were dying, and there were piles of harvest that had not yet been stored. Then he saw the silo: four stone footprints, high and proud.

In the distance, Momma, Buck, and Libby were working in the fields. Even from far away, Arlo could see that they were tired. He started to walk a little faster.

Momma paused from her work and saw a strong, confident dinosaur walking toward the farm. "Henry?" she said, confused.

As Arlo stepped out into the light, Momma's face lit up. "Arlo!" she shouted, running toward him. "ARLO!"

She hugged her son as Buck and Libby ran in from the fields. The family embraced, crying tears of joy. Arlo was finally home.

"Where have you been?" Momma cried. She took a step back and looked at her son in astonishment. She couldn't believe her eyes.

22

As the sun set over the snowcapped peaks of Clawtooth Mountain, the family's silo stood proudly in front of the farmhouse. A fifth stone with a mud footprint had been put up among the four others, making it complete. Arlo had earned his mark, and it was right beside Poppa's. He had done something big for something bigger than himself. And he had made it home.

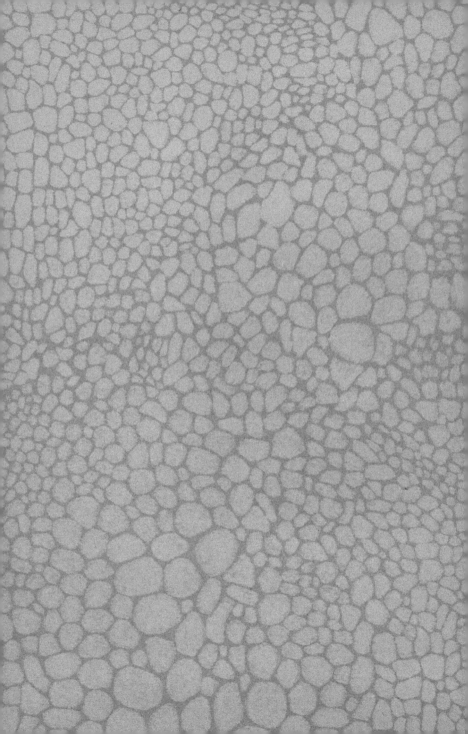

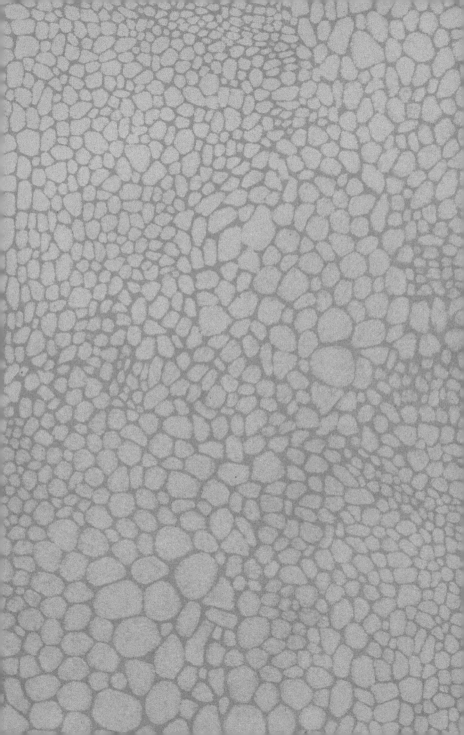

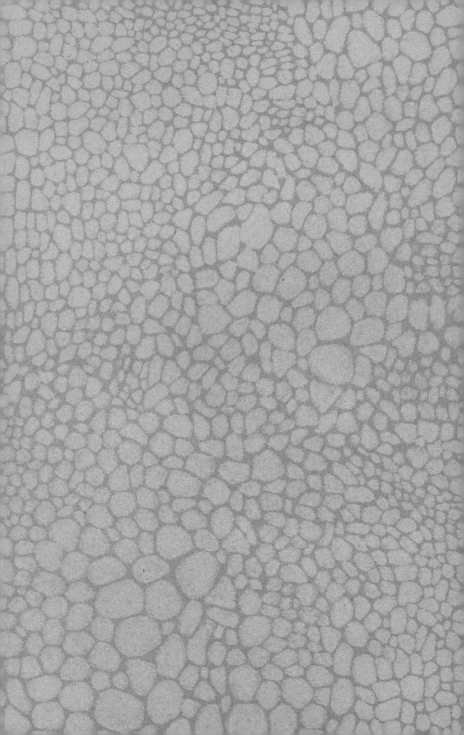